DICTIONARY OF 1000 ROOMS

BY MICHAEL DAHL

Illustrated by
Bradford Kendall

Raintree

www.raintreepublishers.co.uk
Visit our website to find out
more information about
Raintree books.

To order:
☎ Phone 0845 6044371
🖶 Fax +44 (0) 1865 312263
✉ Email myorders@raintreepublishers.co.uk

Customers from outside the UK please telephone +44 1865 312262

Raintree is an imprint of Capstone Global Library Limited, a company
incorporated in England and Wales having its registered office at 7 Pilgrim
Street, London, EC4V 6LB – Registered company number: 6695582

Text © Stone Arch Books 2012
First published in the United Kingdom in hardback and paperback by
Capstone Global Library Ltd in 2012
The moral rights of the proprietor have been asserted.

Art Director: Kay Fraser
Graphic Designer: Hilary Wacholz
Production Specialist: Michelle Biedscheid
Originated by Capstone Global Library Ltd
Printed and bound in China by Leo Paper Products Ltd

ISBN 978 1 406 23698 9 (paperback)
15 14
10 9 8 7 6 5 4 3

British Library Cataloguing in Publication Data
A full catalogue record for this book is available from the British Library.

Contents

Behold the Library of Doom! The world's
largest collection of deadly and dangerous
books. Only the Librarian can prevent
these books from falling into the hands
of those who would use them for evil.

CAN THE LIBRARIAN BE DEFEATED BY
MERE WORDS . . . ?

Chapter 1

FORTRESS

A lone figure CLIMBS a mountain trail, fighting the snow and freezing wind.

It is the <u>Librarian</u>.

He has been climbing the trail all night. The blizzard **ROARS** around him.

Suddenly, the wind **STOPS**.

The snow **FALLS** gently to the ground.

The first ray of morning **SUN** touches the mountainside.

The Librarian wipes the snow and **ICE** from his glasses.

He sees a dark shape up ahead. It rises towards the snowy clouds.

As the Librarian gets closer, he sees that the shape is a vast

FORTRESS.

The fortress is built of **gleaming** metal.

The cold metal walls form the outline of a **GIGANTIC** book.

Giant letters CURVE along the book's spine.

Diction Aerie? wonders the Librarian. *Dictionary?*

Hundreds of open doorways pierce the metal walls.

HA!

Before the Librarian takes another step, he hears laughter.

HA

HA!

HA!

The air grows warm. A ball of red light forms in front of him.

A man stands within the red **GLOW**.

The man wears a metal suit.

A **helmet** with sharp metal horns covers his head.

His gloved hand holds a **blazing** sword.

"I hoped you would find me," the man says. "But you will never find your **PAGES**. You are too late!"

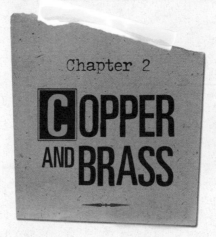

Chapter 2

COPPER AND BRASS

"Stand aside, Wordsmith," says the Librarian.

The **GLOWING** warrior raises his sword. He points it at the rising sun.

"There is your real **enemy**," says the Wordsmith.

foe

adversary

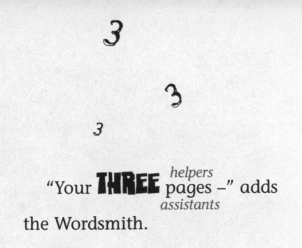

"Your **THREE** _helpers_ pages –" adds _assistants_ the Wordsmith.

"My three young friends," says the Librarian.

"– are trapped within the **maze** of my metal **aerie**," says the warrior.

"It is a **FORTRESS** of copper and brass built by my brother, the Forger, and me," the warrior adds.

"What does the **SUN** have to do with it?" asks the Librarian.

The Wordsmith smiles.

"As the Sun rises, the metal walls of
climbs

my **FORTRESS** grow warmer," he
ascends

says. He raises his sword over his head.

"At noon, the Sun's **RAYS** will beat

straight down. Anything inside the

fortress will be **roasted** alive!"

"The three pages are trapped in three separate parts of the maze," adds the warrior. "You can't save them all in time."

The Librarian takes a step forward. "Why them?" he demands.

"Because my POWERS are not strong enough to defeat you," says the Wordsmith. "But I can destroy those you
lured
care about. That is why I tricked your
snared
pages into coming here."

The ball of red light begins to pulse.

"And with four fewer people guarding the Library of Doom," says the warrior, "its defences are no match for my weapons."

The glowing ball **EXPLODES**.

For a second the snow is the colour of blood.

Then the Wordsmith is gone.

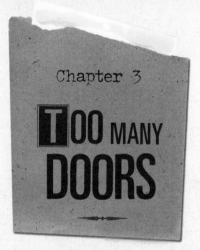

Chapter 3

TOO MANY DOORS

The Librarian stares at the gleaming metal fortress.

Its eastern walls are turning gold in the morning sunlight. He looks at the hundreds of doorways that pierce the walls.

There are so many entries in his diction aerie, thinks the Librarian. *Which one do I choose?*

Quickly, the Librarian **flies** towards the fortress. "One entrance is as good as any other," he says to himself.

He soars through a doorway several stories above the ground.

He lands in a long **METAL** hallway.

The Librarian **flies** through door after door.

Each door leads to another hallway. Each hallway is filled with more doors.

As he flies, he can feel the air GROWING warmer. *The Sun is rising,* he thinks.

"I'll never find them by sight," says the Librarian. "I'll have to use my other senses."

The Librarian is still. He listens for any sound of his pages.

His ears **tingle**. Someone is breathing not too far away.

The Librarian flies down the hallway. He stops at a **HEAVY** brass door.

He touches it with a finger, and the door **BLASTS** open.

Chapter 4
THE FIRST PAGE

"Librarian!" **SHOUTS** a young man.

"Fox!" replies the Librarian. "Hang on! I'll have you **free** in a second."

The young man, Fox, is one of the Librarian's trusted assistants. He is **chained** to the wall.

"Careful!" Fox warns.

Suddenly, another **METAL** door slides into place.

The Librarian is trapped inside.

The Librarian sees **LARGE** letters stamped on the walls of the room.

The walls begin to close in.

"It's the Wordsmith's printing press," says the young page. "We'll be **crushed** flat!"

The Librarian rushes to Fox. He snaps open the **chains**.

The walls move closer.

The hero holds out his hands. "Stop the press!" commands the Librarian.

He points to six of the letters. They
burn **BRIGHTLY** and fly off the
walls.

"Read them out ," commands the Librarian.

Fox reads them in order.

"I am an escapee!" he says.

Instantly, he disappears from the room.

He **reappears** in the hall,

standing safely beside the Librarian.

"That was amazing," says Fox.

"Sometimes reading can **SAVE**

your life," says the Librarian. "Now,

let's go find the others."

Chapter 5

THE FORGER

A light gleams at the end of the hallway.

"Look!" says Fox. "The Wordsmith!"

A man wearing GOLDEN ARMOUR strides down the hall.

"No," says the Librarian. "Someone else."

Clank! Clank!

The man in **GOLD** marches closer.

"Stay where you are!" commands

the Librarian. "You can't stop us."

"I don't want to stop you," says the man. "I want to **HELP** you."

"Who are you?" asks Fox.

"I'm the brother of the one who trapped you here," says the man in GOLD. "They call me the Forger."

The Librarian sees chains attached to the man's feet.

The golden links reach all the way down the hall.

"You are a PRISONER, too," says the Librarian.

The Forger nods. "Free me from this PRISON and I will tell you where your friends are," he says.

"Tell me where they are first," says the Librarian.

"Free me first," says the Forger.

"What if he is lying?" asks Fox.

The Librarian notices that Fox is sweating.

The walls of the hallway are glowing.

The air is **HOT** and **heavy**.

"No one can lie inside the Diction Aerie," says the Forger. "All words are true here."

He stares at the **GLOWING** walls.

"The sun is rising higher," says the Forger. "If we don't move quickly, the other two pages will burn!"

The Librarian raises his hands. Two sharp pieces of paper fly from the ends of his sleeves.

The paper cutters **whirl** around the Forger's chains. Link by link, the chains are **chopped** into small pieces.

"Keep your END of the bargain,
Forger," says the Librarian. "Where are
the two pages?"

The Forger points towards another
doorway.

"That leads outside," he says. "Fly to
the TALLEST tower. You will find a page
there."

"Only one?" asks the Librarian.

"Only one page. Another is **locked** in the dungeon," says the Forger.

"I'll free him," says Fox.

He **HOPS** from one foot to the other. The copper floor is growing warmer.

"Go to the **TOWER**," says the Forger.
"I will go to the dungeon."

The Librarian and Fox run down the
hall leading outside.

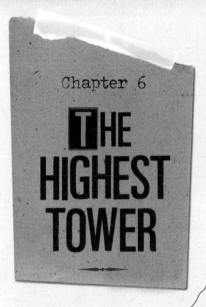

Chapter 6

THE HIGHEST TOWER

The Librarian **soars** above the fortress. Fox clings to his back.

"Over there!" shouts Fox, pointing.

Seven brass **TOWERS** rise from the roof of the fortress.

Fox points to the **highest** one.

"No, that's the highest one, over there," says the Librarian.

He points at a different **TOWER**.

Fox stares at the towers. "They're moving up and down," he says.

"There's **NO** way to tell which one is the highest one!" Fox yells.

"I don't like this," says the Librarian.

He *rushes* like a comet to each moving tower. All of them are **EMPTY**.

"Wait!" cries Fox. "What's that?"

?

?

The Librarian and Fox land on one of the rising and falling **TOWERS**.

Fox bends down and picks up a sheet.

"It's a **PAGE!**" says Fox. "Not a human page! The Forger tricked us!"

"He didn't lie," says the Librarian. "He told the truth, but he picked his words carefully."

The Librarian smiled. "We are heading to the dungeon next!" he says.

"But the forger can't be trusted," says Fox.

"Remember his words," says the Librarian. "He said, 'I will tell you where your friends are.'"

"But no one was in the TOWER," says Fox.

"So that means they must be in the dungeon," says the Librarian.

Fox looks up. "The **SUN** is almost overhead," he says.

They **fly** to the base of the fortress.

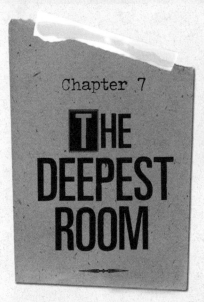

Chapter 7

THE DEEPEST ROOM

Sunlight **reflects** off the Librarian's dark glasses. It flashes onto the bottom wall of the fortress.

The dungeon's copper wall MELTS.

The Forger is inside the dungeon.

He is **unwinding** a huge metal crank.

The chains from the crank are
attached to two gold cages.

He is lowering the cages into two
round holes in the floor.

The other two pages are **locked**
within the lowering cages.

"You were right," says Fox to the Librarian. "The Forger didn't lie. He said he'd go to the dungeon. He didn't say he would rescue our friends."

"My brother told me to delay you," says the Forger. "It would give him more time to **BREAK** into the Library of Doom!"

"His time is up!" says the Librarian.

The Librarian stares at the Forger's metal feet. The sunlight flashes off his glasses again.

FWOOSH!

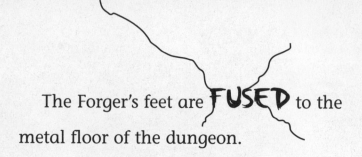

The Forger's feet are **FUSED** to the metal floor of the dungeon.

Fox frees his two friends.

"Hurry!" says the Librarian. "Climb into one of the cages!"

He grabs the top of the cage and flies out of the **broiling** fortress.

They **soar** back towards the Library of Doom.

"I'll finish the Wordsmith as easily as I **DEFEATED** his lying brother," says the Librarian.

4

2

3

1

"And you can **count** on that," Fox tells the other two pages. "The Librarian is a man of his words."

Author

Michael Dahl is the author of more than 200 books for children and young adults. He has won the AEP Distinguished Achievement Award three times for his non-fiction. His Finnegan Zwake mystery series was shortlisted twice by the Anthony and Agatha awards. He has also written the Dragonblood series. He is a featured speaker at conferences on graphic novels and high-interest books for boys.

Illustrator

Bradford Kendall has enjoyed drawing for as long as he can remember. As a boy, he loved to read comic books and watch old monster films. He graduated from university with a BFA in Illustration. He has owned his own commercial art business since 1983, and lives with his wife, Leigh, and their two children, Lily and Stephen. They also have a cat named Hansel and a dog named Gretel.

Glossary

aerie place where a predator waits

defences weapons

dungeon underground prison

escapee someone who escapes

fortress protected and strong building

fused melted with heat and joined

page assistant or helper

pierce make a hole in something

printing press machine that prints text onto paper

pulse blink, beat, or throb steadily

spine part of a book that connects the front and back cover

vast huge

warrior someone who fights

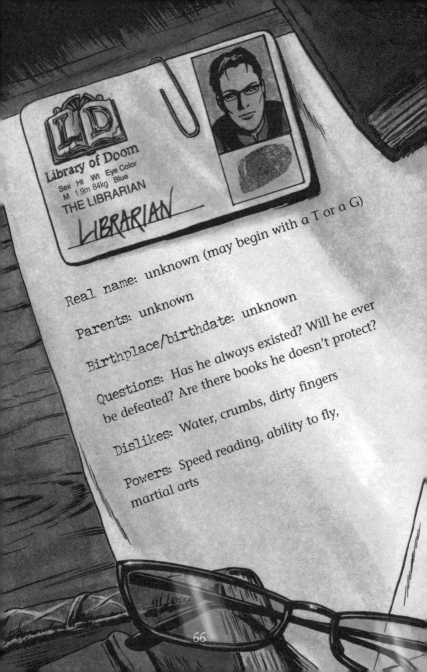

LD

Library of Doom

Sex Ht Wt Eye Color
M 1.9m 84kg Blue

THE LIBRARIAN

LIBRARIAN

Real name: unknown (may begin with a T or a G)

Parents: unknown

Birthplace/birthdate: unknown

Questions: Has he always existed? Will he ever be defeated? Are there books he doesn't protect?

Dislikes: Water, crumbs, dirty fingers

Powers: Speed reading, ability to fly, martial arts

Library of Doom

Sex Ht Wt Eye Color
F 1.7m 68kg Brown
THE SKYWRITER

Skywriter

Real name: Sophia (last name unknown)

Parents: unknown

Birthplace/birthdate: United Kingdom, 20th century

Questions: What is her role in protecting the Librarian? Can she be stopped?

Dislikes: Bad listeners

Powers: Ability to fly, does not need sleep, can research anything, good handwriting

The Forger and The Wordsmith

The Forger and the Wordsmith are brothers, but they are constantly battling. For decades, the Forger was imprisoned in the Diction Aerie, a vast fortress that the brothers built together centuries ago.

Though the Wordsmith put his brother in prison, the Forger remained loyal to his family. The Forger relied on his brother when they worked together to try to defeat the Librarian and attack the Library of Doom. In exchange for the Forger's help, the Wordsmith agreed to release him.

The Librarian was able to defeat the Forger, but the Wordsmith was lying when he said he'd attack the Library. He is still at large.

Discussion questions

1. The Librarian's pages help him in the library. What kinds of things do you think they do? Talk about the different jobs people might have in the **LIBRARY OF DOOM**.

2. How do you think the pages arrived at the Diction Aerie? How did the Forger bring them there? Discuss.

3. The word pages has more than one meaning. In small groups or with a partner, make a list of other words that have more than one meaning.

Writing prompts

1. If you worked in the Library of Doom, what JOB would you want to have? Write about it.

2. Try writing this story from one of the PAGES' point of view. What does that person experience?

3. The WORDSMITH and the Forger are brothers. Write about someone in your family. What do you like or dislike about that person?

More books from the Library of Doom

Return to the Library of Doom